Young Learner's

Stories from Around the World

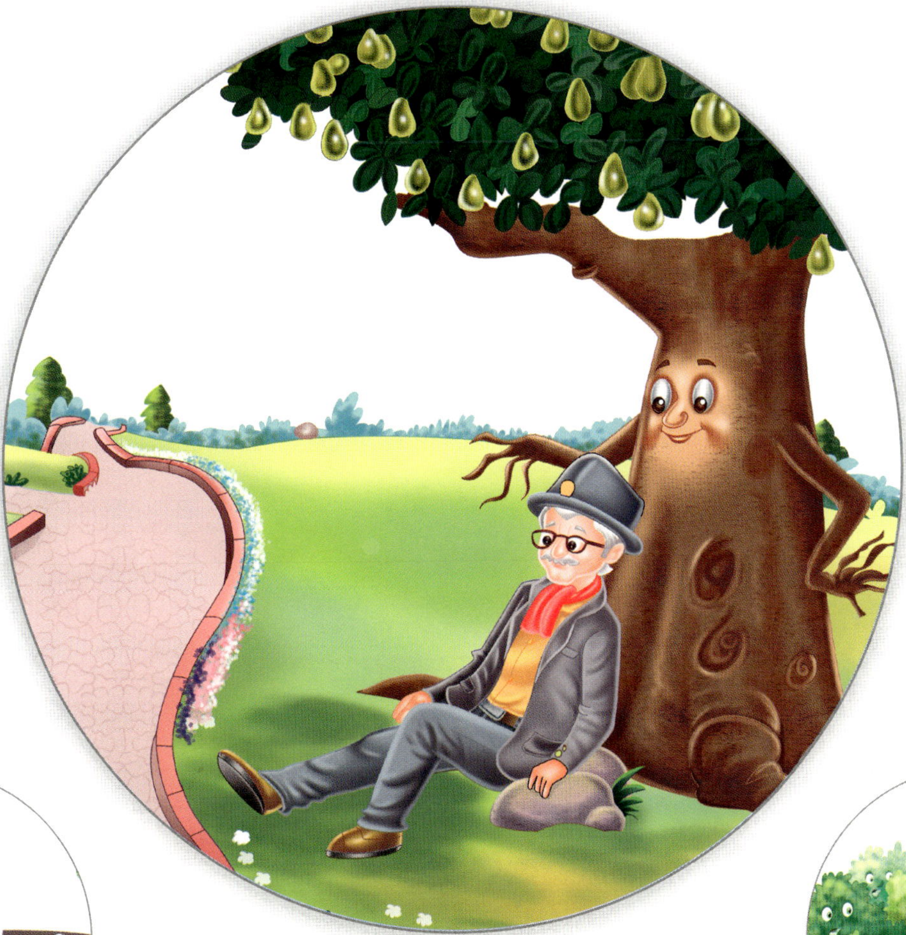

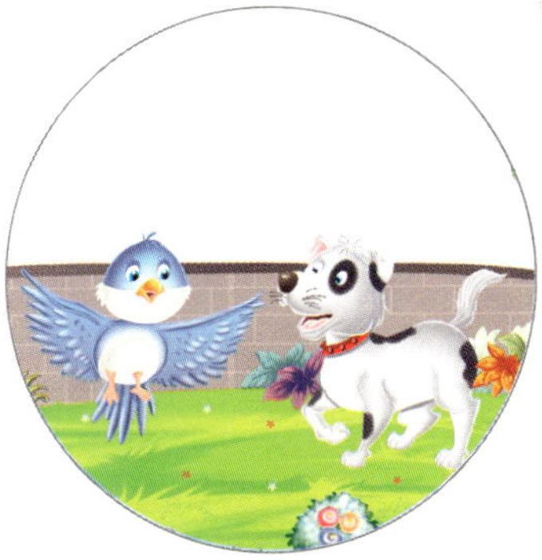

The Envious Dog

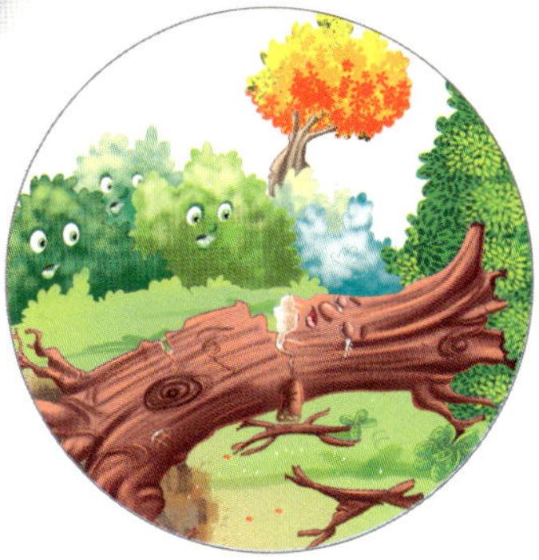

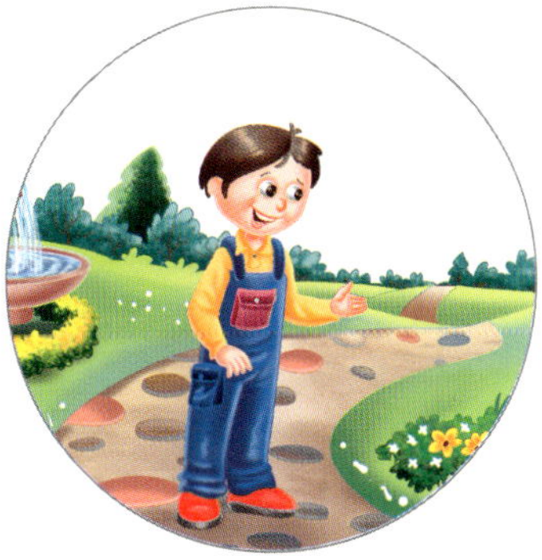

The Ungrateful Boy

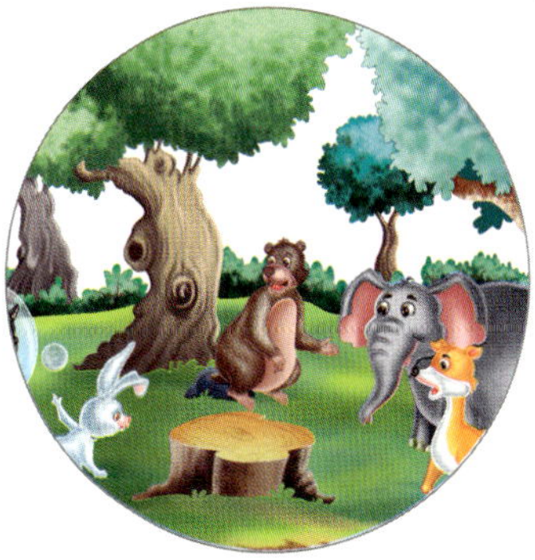

True Friends

The Boastful Tree

The Envious Dog

(A story from Africa)

One fine afternoon, Timmy the dog, was roaming around in the garden, looking here and there. He saw a cat sitting on the high boundary wall of the garden. He wondered how nice it would be to climb up the high wall.

He thought to himself, "If only I could climb as high as the cat, I would be able to see even the distant objects."

Sighing, he walked a little ahead and saw pretty fishes in the pond. He thought, “It would be so nice to live in the pond and have fun swimming all day long.”

Just then, he heard one fish say to the other, “The grass looks so nice and warm. It is so boring to swim all the time. I wish I could leave this water and relax on the soft green grass.”

After some time, a bird came flying. Now, Timmy wished that he too could fly!

Seeing Timmy relaxing on the green grass, the bird said to him, “I wish I could play and roll all day long in the grass just like you. I am so tired of flapping my wings all the time.”

Having heard the fishes and the bird, Timmy realised that it was foolish to be wanting to be someone else. We should all learn to be happy with the way we are. We should be thankful to God for making each one of us special and different.

The Ungrateful Boy

(A story from England)

A huge pear tree stood in the middle of a garden. A little boy named John often played around it. As John grew older, he stopped visiting the tree. One day, he was playing with his friends when the tree called out to him, "John, come and play here. Spend some time with me. I am also your friend." John replied, "I do not wish to play with you. If you are my friend then give me money to buy new toys."

The tree said, "You can sell my pears and buy toys with that money." John quickly gathered as many pears as he could and left happily.

Many years went by and John grew up to be a tall and handsome young man. One day, he went to the same garden. The tree asked him to spend some time with him.

John said, “I do not have time to sit and chat with you. I need wood to repair my house.”

The tree smiled and said, “Chop off my branches and take as much wood as you want for the repairs.”

So, John chopped off the branches and left, without even bothering to thank the tree.

More years went by and John was an old man now. His back was bent and he walked very slowly. One day, he went to the same garden for a walk. The tree was excited to see him, and asked him to rest under its leafy branches.

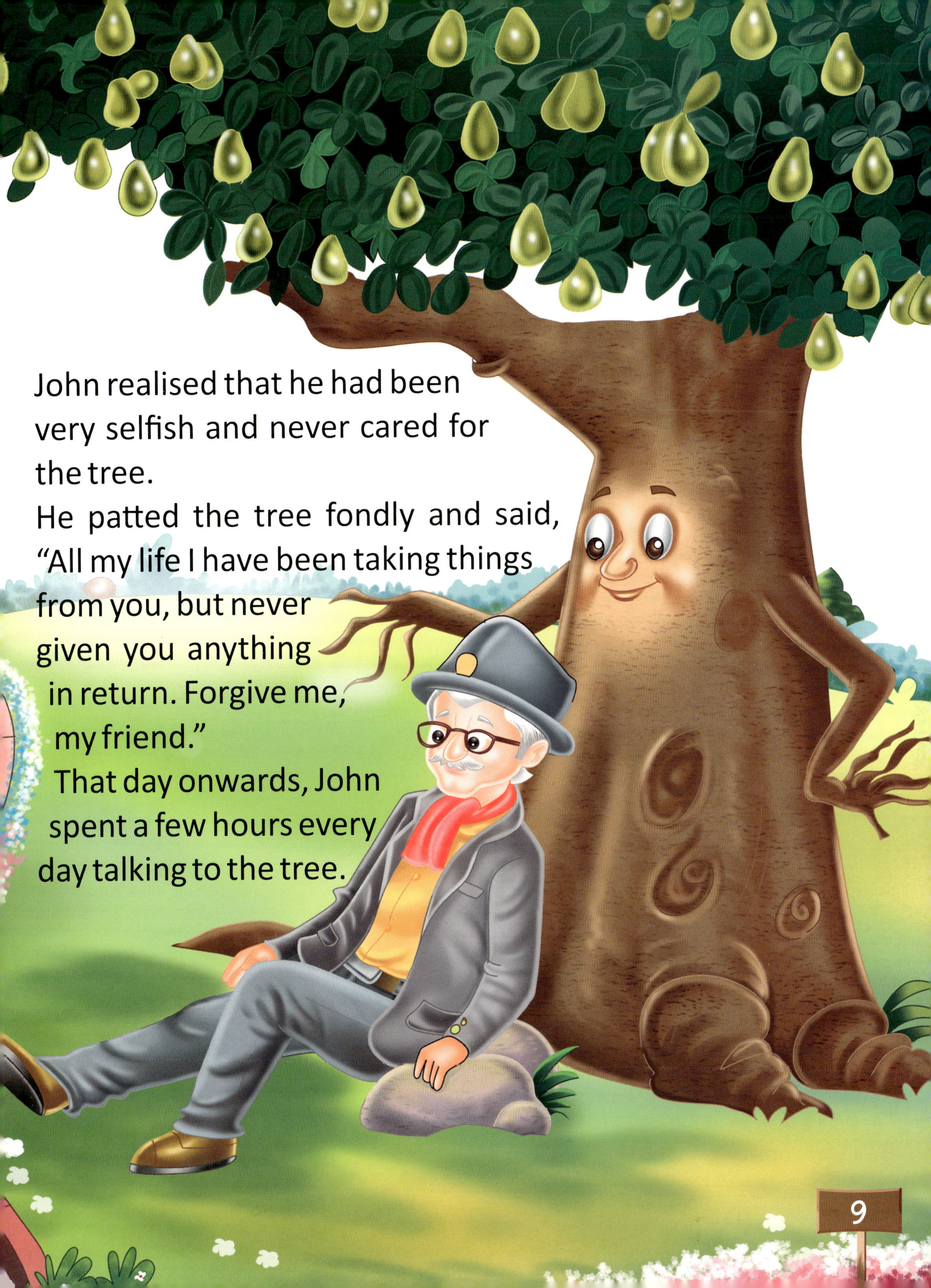

John realised that he had been very selfish and never cared for the tree.

He patted the tree fondly and said, "All my life I have been taking things from you, but never given you anything in return. Forgive me, my friend."

That day onwards, John spent a few hours every day talking to the tree.

True Friends

(A story from America)

Harry the hare lived in a forest. He had many friends and they played together all day long. He always helped them when they were in need. He and his friends often made fun of the two porcupine sisters, Paula and Pearly, who also lived in the forest. They called them names like spiny, prickly and needles and laughed at them. One day, Harry heard that wild dogs had come to the forest and wanted to make a meal out of him. He was very scared. He ran to Danny the deer to ask for his help.

But Danny refused to help him, saying he was busy. So, Harry went to ask Barny the bear for help. “Please save me from the wild dogs, Barny!” said Harry. But Barny refused him too, saying he had to clean his den. Next, Harry asked Ellie the elephant for help. Ellie refused to help him saying that she had to take care of her children.

Harry then went to Manny the monkey, Gabby the goat and Penny the pig. But no one helped him. Each one came up with an excuse. Harry felt very sad and betrayed. The truth was that all the animals were scared of the wild dogs.

Seeing him alone, the wild dogs tried to attack him. Harry ran for his life. The wild dogs had almost caught him when Paula and Pearly came to his rescue.

They scared the dogs away with their thorny spines. Harry thanked them for having saved his life. From that day onwards, Harry spent all his time with Paula and Pearly. He had realised that only those who help us in times of need are our true friends.

The Boastful Tree

(A story from Japan)

Once upon a time, there was a proud tree. He was tall and strong unlike the small bushes that grew around him. The tall tree told the bushes, “I am big and powerful. Look at you. You all are so short and weak. How I pity you all!” The old wise bush replied, “Dear friend, too much pride does no good. The proud often fall, and the humble survive. Sometimes in life, we have to adjust with the circumstances.”

The tree ignored the bush's wise words and kept praising himself. Whenever strong winds blew, the tree would stand erect and tall. Even when it rained, he stood strong. At the same time, the bushes would often get bent for their stems were weak and thin. The strong tree made fun of their fragile bodies.

One day, a storm began to blow. As the storm grew stronger, the bushes gave in to the fury of the nature and bowed low. However, the tree resisted and stood facing the storm, refusing to bend even a bit. The storm grew stronger and stronger. The tree was no match for the mighty storm, and he came crashing down.

When the storm was over, the bushes straightened up. They felt sorry for the fallen tree, whose pride had been in vain.